OLLIE FORGOT

OLLIE FORGOT

by Tedd Arnold

SCHOLASTIC INC.
New York   Toronto   London   Auckland   Sydney
Mexico City   New Delhi   Hong Kong

For my wife, Carol

ISBN 0-590-51906-9

Copyright © 1988 by Tedd Arnold. All rights reserved.
Published by Scholastic Inc., 555 Broadway, New York, NY 10012,
by arrangement with Dial Books for Young Readers,
a division of Penguin Putnam Inc.
SCHOLASTIC and associated logos are trademarks and/or registered
trademarks of Scholastic Inc.

12 11 10 9 8 7 6 5 4 3 2 1   8 9/9 0 1 2 3/0

Printed in the U.S.A.   08

First Scholastic printing, December 1998

Design by Nancy R. Leo

The artwork was prepared using colored pencils
and watercolor washes. It was then color-separated and reproduced
as red, blue, yellow, and black halftones.

Ollie was a good boy, but he had one big problem. He was very forgetful. He even had trouble remembering the last words anyone said to him.

One day his mother gave him three coins and sent him to market for:

"A joint of beef, a wedge of cheese,
A loaf of bread, too, if you please."

Afraid he might forget his mother's words, Ollie walked off, saying loudly over and over,

"A joint of beef, a wedge of cheese,
A loaf of bread, too, if you please.
A joint of beef, a wedge of cheese…"

Soon after he left the house, a terrible storm blew up. Ollie was so startled by the first clap of thunder, he forgot his mother's words, and an old rhyme popped into his head:

"Rain, rain, go away.
Come again another day."

But Ollie didn't let a little rain stop him. He walked on down the road until he met a farmer working in his wheat field. All the while Ollie kept repeating,

"Rain, rain, go away.
Come again another day."

It had been a very dry season, and the farmer was hoping for more rain. Ollie's words made him angry, and he chased the boy, shouting,

"I hope it rains a long, long while,
And as it rains I'll sing and smile."

Ollie outran the farmer but began saying the farmer's words because they were all he could remember. Soon he came to a man whose house was flooded by rain. Ollie kept repeating,

"I hope it rains a long, long while,
And as it rains I'll sing and smile."

The man had been hoping the rain would soon stop. When he heard Ollie's words, he became furious and ran after the boy, crying,

"Your words are foolish as can be.
A kick is what you need from me."

Away Ollie ran, not knowing what he had done. By and by
he came upon a minstrel singing love songs for pennies. Ollie
kept saying over and over,

"Your words are foolish as can be.
A kick is what you need from me."

This outraged the minstrel, who had been singing a very beautiful verse. He beat poor Ollie with his lute and shouted:

"I'd give my coins, though they are few,
If I could get my hands on you."

Ollie quickly escaped, but he remembered the minstrel's words. Farther along the road a girl was selling puppies from a wagon. As Ollie petted one of the pups he said,

"I'd give my coins, though they are few,
    If I could get my hands on you."

All day the girl had been trying to sell the three puppies. She thought she finally had a paying customer, so she promptly spoke up, not wanting the other two puppies left behind:

"Two more pups looking for a home.
Two more pups begging for a bone."

Foolishly Ollie gave the girl his coins and carried away all the puppies. Soon he came to a church where a man and a woman were being wed. Again and again he repeated,

"Two more pups looking for a home.
Two more pups begging for a bone."

The man and woman were furious that the boy would insult
them in such a way. They leaped at Ollie, crying out,

"That child is such a lowly beast,
And not deserving in the least."

Poor Ollie ran away without looking back, not once under-
standing why everyone was so angry with him. Suddenly he
came upon a mother and baby while he was repeating,

"That child is such a lowly beast,
And not deserving in the least."

The young mother at once scolded the bad-mouthed boy and
wagged her finger at him, saying,

"Hold your tongue now, if you can.
You should get on home, young man."

Finally Ollie came to the market. He had three puppies, no money, and no idea why he was there.

Among the crowds was a gentleman so busy giving a speech,
he had not noticed his house was on fire. Ollie repeated the
only words he could remember:

"Hold your tongue now, if you can.
You should get on home, young man."

Hearing Ollie's words, the man looked up quickly and ran to save his house from burning. He rewarded Ollie with ten gold coins and invited him to a feast of:

"A joint of beef, a wedge of cheese,
A loaf of bread, too, if you please."

Suddenly Ollie remembered his mother's words. Afraid he might forget again, he did not stay to eat. He thanked the man and went directly to the grocer, where he purchased:

"A joint of beef, a wedge of cheese,
A loaf of bread, too, if you please."

Then Ollie tried to remember his way home.